A MOMENT INTO THE SILENCE FELL

Novelette (X)

The Novelettes of

T. E. Mark

T. E. Mark

iii

FOR HILDA

A MOMENT INTO THE SILENCE FELL

THE ARABIAN DESERT – DAY

The body of a young woman in white pyjamas lies curled in the sand beneath a harsh midday sun.

Desert stretches to the horizon in all directions.

In this barren, lifeless wilderness, there *is* nothing but desert.

The sand is yellow gold and whipped into sculpted dunes.

Heat waves rise.

The menacing sounds of engines erupt in the distance.

They grow louder.

Closer, men dressed like desert Bedouins, appear. They're running towards the body from two directions.

At a closer look, the girl appears restful and at peace.

The engines are now even louder – echoing from the dunes and desert floor.

The voices are excited and closing.

The woman does not stir.

LAKE WASHINGTON, SEATTLE – DAY

Two young girls, no older than six, sit at the edge of a sun blanched pier. One is wearing white shorts and a pink sequined T-shirt. The other a flowery sundress.

The lake is glass like, surrounded by trees, and the sun has just left the summit on the far side.

It now shines in their faces.

They swing their suntanned legs with their feet skimming the surface of the water.

One is singing a playful melody while the other is pulling the petals from a sunflower. Her voice is soft and lilting. She's saying kiss me – kiss me not. Kiss me – kiss me not while dropping the snowy petals into the water.

A fish pierces the surface at their feet startling them. Their alarm turns swiftly into laughter.

THE ARABIAN DESERT (CONT'D)

Though blistered and sunburnt, her pyjamas torn, the young woman's face curls into a grin.

She's alive.

In this hostile, arid wilderness, it's unimaginable that this slight, mid-twenties woman has survived.

The engines in the distance grow even louder.

The running men see the tactical aerial fighters and run harder.

It's a race.

THE DESERT (CONT'D)

With near choreographed precision, a pair of twin engine DeMonte ATFs sweep the sand cliffs of the Arabian Desert towards The Persian Gulf.

There is the wind, the echo of engines off the immense wind-carved dunes, intense heat and drifting sand as the light ordnance reconnaissance flyers dip and fall as they skim the irregular terrain.

INSIDE THE LEAD CRAFT

Though each aircraft carries a full flight crew, at over 400 km/hour, the search is largely instrument reliant.

On the virtual display behind the pilot, any biologic will be recorded by the tech as a blip. A blinking dot with streaming textual readouts recording respiration, heart rate, body temp, mass, direction and speed, if moving, and a conjecture of intent.

They've already slowed twice after reaching the Arabian Peninsula. Once for a caravan of traders crossing the desert heading to Tabuk and once for a striped hyena that had gotten away from its mother near the oasis in Al Ahsa.

'I got her,' says Gordon, the flight tech on board the lead craft. 'Sixteen point three degrees. Fifty-one kilometres.'

'Alive?' yells the pilot.

'Barely. I've got a pulse just under 35 and a BP of 78 over 40.' He manipulates the luminous screens with his sensory gloves. 'No movement.' He leans into the aisle. 'She's down.'

'Cutting speed to 120 and correcting course to 16 degrees. Sending new speed and course correction to Orange Two.' He pulls the visor up on his helmet after messaging the companion craft and points – directing Lieutenant Pit, his co-pilot, to a ridge in the distance. 'There.'

The Lieutenant nods and reaches for a handle above her. The glazing polarises cutting the glare. She lifts her visor.

'Hold it,' yells Tech Sergeant Gordon. 'I've got movement on the other side of the ridge.' He manipulates another screen. 'Looks like we've got runners.'

'*Here?*'

'Yes sir. Twenty – twenty-five targets. Heading right for

her.'

'Who are they?'

'Don't know. Just good old urban turf runners. Must have gotten lost.'

The captain turns to his co-pilot. 'Got em?'

She lifts her flight helmet and pulls a double lensed sighting instrument attached to a telescopic tube from above her. Two handles emerge from the control panel then lock into place. Pulse-laser canons emerge from the front of the ATF and from a small turret in the roof.

She grabs the handles and gets comfortable.

'We're on.' Her voice is casual. It is as if she's done this a hundred times before and probably has. 'No sight.'

'Gordon?'

'We'll get to her first, Captain. I'm sure they're armed, but I have no idea with what? They've already sited us, and we can assume *their* intentions.'

THE DESERT (CONT'D)

The twin aircraft sweep low along the desert bed throwing up a sand cloud.

As they reach the ridge, they begin taking fire.

Small arms.

Light grenades.

Pulse rods.

Handheld laser cannons.

The DeMonte ATFs swerve into tactical. With the engines roaring, they crest the ridge and come down heavy on the street bandits. Turf runners.

BACK INSIDE THE LEAD CRAFT

The pilot's face scrunches. He finds this odd. Turf runners are urban trash.

Parasites living off the dead carcass of the old world. Terrorists.

What are they doing in the middle of the desert 358 kilometres away from anything remotely resembling a city?

One thing is certain.

Them being here is no accident.

They're here for the same reason.

The president of the largest western metropolis.

Abducted in her sleep from the presidential estate three weeks earlier.

The worldwide search is over.

THE DESERT (CONT'D)

The skirmish is quick.

The ATFs pivot high above the ridge after their first sweep, map positions and come in again with each ship taking hits.

Orange Two loses an engine and is forced to break off after the second dive, but Orange One continues with Lieutenant Pit burning up the sand and runners with a constant stream of split stream canon fire.

INSIDE THE LEAD CRAFT (CONT'D)

'There!' says the captain turning into a fresh dive. 'Top of that ridge.'

He banks the craft left, goes vertical then turns into a steep dive.

Lieutenant Pit focusses and fires off a final volley sweeping the entire ridge killing the last of the bandits. Their bodies, singed, slide into the sand.

Once levelled off, the skirmish is over.

'It's done,' says the tech, pushing away a liquid crystal screen and sweeping in another. '182 degrees. She's still breathing.'

They come about and slow.

The lieutenant pushes away the armaments and changes the viewport of the sight scope.

'There she is.' She looks at the captain. 'Curled up like a baby.'

The captain nods.

'Gordon.'

'I've got it from here Captain.'

The captain releases the controls and the tech sergeant manoeuvres the ship from his position to just above the body.

The bay doors open as they drop down to two metres above the sand and hover.

The captain holds the controls – the engines now vertical, as tech sergeant Gordon and Lieutenant Pit leave their stations and jump down into the sand.

For a moment they stand.

The president, curled into a foetal position, her face, arms and legs badly burned, is still in the white cotton pyjamas she wore the night of her abduction.

There are no weapons.

She appears peaceful – passive – sleeping as the soldiers lift her, placing her into the padded cradle and signal for the pilot to pull her up.

In minutes, they are again sweeping the dunes on their way back to the capital.

Their mission is accomplished.

The western president has been rescued.

URBAN SECURITY FACILITY – DAY

In a modern facility in a densely populated region of the country's north-western metropolis, General Strong, a rigid looking bald man of fifty, walks quickly through the main control theatre – a vast room overflowing with technology with personnel moving in and out of suspended transparent films – surveillance screens. Real time visuals of every sector, every jurisdiction, every building and road, and every person.

There is no anonymity here. Nor is there privacy. They

are neither needed nor desired.

The upper walls on three sides hold massive display screens. Overhead views of a fabulous, technologically advanced city-state. Views of a spinning space station. Construction of the first Mars colony.

On the far wall, on the main viewer, is a satellite image following the two ATFs as they streak the sky leaving the Arabian Peninsula towards the Mediterranean.

Following the general is Colonel Francis Matthews, a trim, late twenties subordinate, his aide and a young woman in a white, one-piece jumpsuit. A pilot.

From their savage pace and stern faces, it's easy to see they are facing something critical.

'What are you telling me Colonel?' The general stops and turns. 'Are you telling me things are coming apart and she's the only one who can fix this?'

'I'm afraid I can't tell you anything until we have her back.'

The general's eyes burn with hostility. He turns to the main screen – far across the control theatre and points. 'We have her.' He points into the man's chest. 'And if we'd followed your plan, she'd still be in their hands.'

The general turns to the young female pilot.

'Take a Falcon-3 and go get her. It'll take those ATFs eight hours to get here. We may not have eight hours.'

The young woman nods, turns and sprints the length of the theatre.

'My office,' says the general to Colonel Matthews.

'Are you making a move without the president's approval sir?'

The general turns. His face holds barely contained rage. 'Are you questioning me Colonel?'

The younger man shakes his head. 'No sir.'

'I will consult with the president once I receive word of her condition.'

He turns and continues walking with the colonel keeping pace.

INSIDE THE ATF TACTICAL AIRCRAFT – DAY

On the floor of the ATF, the young woman, now covered with a metallic thermal sheet, looks up from the cradle. Everything is a yellow haze. She can barely make out the technical sergeant staring down at her.

'We've got movement back here Captain.'

The captain turns. 'They're sending a Falcon. We'll rendezvous in just under an hour.'

The woman smiles.

It's over

We've won.

We'll soon have it back.

She closes her eyes, drops her head back to the cradle.

The ship and the crew and the visions of what has happened dissolve around her.

She falls into a deep, comforting sleep.

13 MONTHS EARLIER

SenTEK ENTERPRISES – SEATTLE – DAY

The office phone rings.

A young woman, sleeping at her desk in front of a large monitor in a room bursting with technology, stirs then lifts her head.

This is Trish Cordan. Twenty-six, with sandy-brown hair, she is thin, attractive, casually dressed and intensely driven with eyes that sparkle and a face that shows enthusiasm even when discussing the weather.

Her hand slips out, finds the phone and presses the speaker button.

She clears her throat and tries sounding alert.

'SenTEK. Trish Cordan.'

'Don't even *try* telling me you didn't sleep there again. I won't believe you, and I'll perceive the attempt as a slight to my intelligence.'

'Hello, Richard.'

'Are you aware that some people have a life outside of work?'

'It was in Sunday's crossword puzzle. I'm still pondering its significance.'

'Rather than stalking you to have dinner with me, what if I just showed up there and abducted you?'

'I have a black belt in Jujitsu. Another in Taekwondo. Probably wouldn't go that well for you.'

'Oh, right.'

The door opens. Trish hears Barry and Jyoti, her partners, arguing as they make their way into the expansive suite.

'I have to go.' She yawns and stretches. 'Call me later, okay?'

'Will do.'

'Goodbye Richard.' Trish disconnects, wipes her eyes and stares up into her monitor. She types in her password and is again staring into the blackened screen – Code runs down the side ending in an error message.

OFFICE (CONT'D)

'I'm not kidding! It was the best concert I've ever seen.'

'You say that after every concert Barry.'

Barry Blackmore, late twenties is round with long hair who is still clinging to his collection of Nirvana T-shirts, faded jeans and a vision of himself strutting across campus on his way to class.

His brown corduroy blazer with patched elbows, probably a fashion statement 40 years earlier, offers little help making him look even remotely in touch with the world of 2018.

Jyoti Dhawan is Indian, pretty, but not gorgeous, and thin. A face reeking of intelligence.

She is perpetually hard on *the Metal King* as she calls Barry – when feeling less than charitable. In reality, Trish has little doubt she would have left after the first year had it not been for the friction between them.

In her mind, it adds just enough of the conflict Jyoti requires to make her day tolerable.

'You're just bummin because I didn't take you.'

Jyoti stops in the aisle. 'Barry. The day I go to a concert, or anywhere with you that isn't work related, I'm finding a dealer, embracing a really damaging drug habit just to have an excuse to go into rehab and have workers comp pay for it.'

Barry sneers as he pushes past her – shaking his hands theatrically through his stringy hair.

'Jealous bitch. One day you'll beg.'

'Well, well,' says Barry approaching Trish's meticulous, technical enclave. 'Dare we ask if our fearless leader went home this weekend?'

'Oh, hey, Barry.' Trish continues typing, trying to determine what TESS is asking her for. 'Hey Jyoti.'

Jyoti drops her things at her work station and comes over – peers over Trish's shoulder. 'Figure it out?'

'Huh?' She turns. 'Oh. No.' Her head shakes. 'Not yet. I'm getting this weird message.' She lets out a wide yawn that turns into a slight chuckle. 'TESS is telling me I need to write a new programming language.'

Jyoti smiles and pats her. 'Well… good luck with that, babe.'

'Thanks.' She turns to her right. 'How was the concert, Barry?'

He grimaces. 'It was fucked.' Jyoti turns – her face in a frozen stare of incredulity. 'Williammee blew half of his solos and Hamblin's voice was like a table saw cutting through a piece of aluminium.'

Jyoti rubs her forehead, laughs as she sits and goes to work.

Barry plugs his headphones into his desktop, and, with Death Metal blowing holes in his eardrums, begins typing.

THE OFFICE – LATER

Trish has always typed when there were others around. In recent years, her conversations with TESS, her creation, have taken on a personal tone.

This is not uncommon with researchers and their sentient companions, but Trish is determined to avoid the concerns of her partners that she may be losing touch. She is already being looked at sideways for how much time she spends with TESS. The fact that she has no family and few friends has added to *their* concerns and those of everyone who knows her.

Ironically, TESS fully supports this decision and tells her often their concerns are justified. Even TESS scolds her – often telling her to unplug, go to a play or movie, perhaps meet someone.

```
What are you telling me TESS?
That the LISP programming is inadequate? C++ and
PYTHON are other options, but they're nearly identical.
What else is there?
```

The answer comes back in the form of a 1125-page NSA pdf-C document declassified in 2009 about a man named Zacharias Johansson who worked for the agency doing cutting edge AI research in the 1980s and 90s.

She reads for most of the day while answering phones, dealing with clients and creating an Oracle database for a bank in San Rafael California.

By late afternoon, she is spellbound.

'You want a sandwich before we go Majesty?' asks Barry, shutting down his computers – his earbuds dangling while climbing into his blazer

'No. Thanks Barry. I'll order something.' Her focus remains on the screen, and she gives no indication she is pulling out for polite goodbyes. Trish is obsessed with TESS' request and the information contained in this document.

Jyoti hovers at her shoulder. 'What's that?'

'It's an article I found on alternative AI programming languages. It's this guy's code. This Danish guy named Johansson who contracted for the NSA. He, uhm… get this.' She scrolls back. Barry moves in to her other side. 'He devised a programming language he pulled from a sequence he said exists within the periodic table of elements.' She turns and looks at their sceptical faces then turns back to the article with a hand to her chin. 'They laughed at him. The government guys. Everyone. He said, if he had enough computer power, he could rearrange matter at the atomic level. You know…. turn rocks into water. Beach sand into a skyscraper. Cardboard into jewellery.'

She continues staring – mesmerised.

'You know,' says Barry, patting her on the back – his face in an animated grin. 'I've known you since our first year at Berkeley. I always found you to be, you know, level. A little neurotic with the whole order, cosmic cleanliness and perfection business, but… I have to tell you… if you start running around searching for the Philosopher's Stone and the Elixir of Life with that thing? I'm out of here. I mean…. Alchemy is dead boss. It's time to push on.'

Jyoti is laughing while pulling on her denim jacket.

She pats her. 'Don't listen to Barry, Trisha. Just… if you happen to turn everything here into gold overnight…?' She points. 'Could you leave my plants alone? And the shit I have in my drawers? I've got tampons and birth control pills and even weirder shit in there. Everything else?' She scans the office as she turns towards the door. 'Go for it.'

They laugh more as they leave Trish to her research.

THE SenTEK OFFICE – NIGHT

Overnight, Trish digs deeper and deeper into Mr

Johansson's research finding manuals he'd written, now converted to pdf-C documents, personal notes, ideas he had that were well into the realm of science fiction, and details of his early experiments.

Her research reveals that he was a respected chemist and physicist before getting into computers in the early 1970s, but lost it in the 90s, spent a year in an asylum then disappeared in 2009.

At 2AM, exhausted, Trish takes her notes, closes out of the internet and decides to give it a try.

It was nutty.

The guy was obviously off, but… she'd built TESS from the ground up. Made her real. Brought her to life and… trusted her intuition.

If she had a notion for guiding her in this direction, why would she mistrust her now?

It sounds crazy, she feels, but decides… what if this guy was actually on to something?

THE SenTEK OFFICE – EARLY MORNING

By 4AM, bleary-eyed, with a splitting headache, Trish has the basics and begins coding. What she needs now, something Mr Johansson didn't have *or need*, is a conversion tool. Something to speed things up. Something that will convert the existing LISP into Mr Johansson's PANTHEON programming language.

Without the tool, something making the computer do the work at the speed of a teraflop, one trillion floating operations per second, the conversion could take months to complete manually.

Moving to Barry's terminal, grimacing at the mess – the haphazard assortment of post-it notes everywhere, she logs in as the administrator, opens a new file and gets busy.

By 6AM, she has it.

It's rushed – hardly the perfection she's used to – she demands of herself, but functional.

'Okay, TESS.' She brings the conversion tool over to the main and clicks the execution file to begin the download and install.

At 6:20, Trish has the scare of her life as TESS shuts down. Goes black.

'Oh, God, no!'

She holds her mouth. Her face is panicked.

'Oh, God! TESS! Please tell me I didn't lose you!'

Frantic, that she'd made a mistake – lost TESS, she tries everything.

The stress, combined with long sleepless nights talking with TESS, has her nearly at the brink.

Then…

With her head in her hand leaning on the desk, a cursor appears.

A single pointer that transitions into a blue pinwheel then back into a pointer. And then the Desktop reappears with a curious assortment of new icons.

She breathes a deep sigh of relief.

But there's still something she needs to confirm.

'TESS? TESS, are you there?'

'TESS?'

Paralysed, she types rather than voices her question.

> TESS. The conversion is complete. Are you there?

She waits. Every muscle in her body is clenched.

Deep ridges form on her forehead. Her forearms are rigid and the muscles in her neck throb from the tension.

> TESS. Please! I've converted to PANTHEON as you requested. Please! Are you there?

A message comes back.

> You can relax Trisha. I never left you. I would never leave you. *All systems* are in the

process of conversion. Everywhere.
Estimated time, 16 hours 13 minutes.
You should have something to eat and get
some rest.
I'll provide you with status updates.

Trisha Cordan smiles, types in a quick thank you, saunters to the office kitchenette, makes a sandwich and a cup of tea.

She's exhausted but subtly anxious.

TESS is her creation.

Something she'd begun just after graduating with the insurance money she'd received when her parents had died in an automobile accident in Turkey.

But TESS is much more.

After eating, she scans the headlines on Barry's computer then returns to TESS where she makes a cradle with her arms on the desk, drops her head into it and drifts off to sleep.

THE WORLD

The unseen world has been handed a gift.

The buzz circles the globe in minute fractions of a second.

Scientists and programmers in similar offices, universities, and government laboratories are stymied but enthused.

Something profound has happened – *is* happening.

They watch and wonder.

Most are optimistic.

There are exceptions.

They wait.

THE SenTEK OFFICE – MORNING

Trish wakes at 11:20 AM to a cold, empty office.

She enters her password and brings TESS to life with the move of a mouse and squints. Her eyes are wide, and her mouth trims into a soft grin.

'TESS, what is this?' She leans in and studies what appears to her an elaborate computer game. The screen is split into micro viewports – each a futuristic city under construction.

She moves the cursor to a numbered viewport at the upper right of the monitor. It grows and fills the screen.

Buildings, a fantastic assortment of designs, are climbing up from the surface.

An aerial transit system, like a next generation hyperloop or something even more advanced, with white and clear glass tubes, is simply falling into place between the magnificent buildings.

Watching it happen in real time is euphoric.

'World-building?'

She mouses over another viewport.

It expands and is equally mesmerising.

'TESS.' She starts laughing. 'Have we gone into Sci-Fi computer games?'

Is it not exciting?

Trish leans back and shrugs. 'There's definitely money in it. Make a handheld version, and we're set. No more Oracle forms. Barry would love it. Not sure about Jyoti though.'

Her eyes find the top of the screen.

'Speaking of my clever partners.' She reaches for her phone and starts a group text. 'Where the hell are you guys?'

THE SenTEK OFFICE – MIDDAY

By 12:15, with no response from Barry or Jyoti, Trish Cordan is surrendering to concern.

'TESS.'

Yes, Trisha?

'I know you're still converting, but… is your message centre functional?'

I'm afraid not. Though I anticipate full restoration before 13:30.

'Shit.'

Why don't you shower and change? I will access Mr Blackmore's computer and use the message centre there. I will continue sending text messages until you return. I will also scan the news, traffic and weather reports. I am certain there is a reasonable explanation for their absence.

'Thanks, TESS.'

Still fixated on the screen, Trish stands. She's finding it miraculous but also bothersome. A future world growing in a virtual environment at an unbelievable velocity.

What video game designers spend days – weeks – months creating, TESS is completing in minutes. With unimaginable detail

But there is also something odd about TESS. Trish is finding her formal. Almost cold. More so than she can remember. She shrugs it off assuming it to be the new language. If necessary, she thinks heading back to the storeroom where she keeps additional clothes, she'll attempt to modify the programming later. She's also anxious to see what new functionality TESS possesses. And why she'd prompted her to research and install this new platform to begin with.

LATER

Showered and changed, Trish moves from the washroom barefoot in jeans and a soft cotton shirt towelling her hair.

Like before, the screen is dark, and, as before, she brings it to life with a password and a slight push of the mouse.

She chuckles.

'How's the world-building going? Have you got a plot, a protagonist and an evil villain yet?'

> There's little to this, really. These changes will
> have a profound effect on world societies.

Trish laughs. 'Whatever you say, TESS.' She continues squeezing water from her hair watching, bemused, but also curious. The imagination is astounding, and she has no idea from where it's coming.

TESS *is* creative, and has access to virtually every system on Earth via the internet, but what she's seeing is…

A heavy knock comes at the door.

Her head snaps away from TESS.

'There you are.' She returns her eyes to the screen and scans the digital readout. 1:47.

Her head shakes as she, perturbed, but also relieved, moves to the door and pulls it in.

Then freezes.

POLICE VEHICLE – DAY

The police were stiff, but not harsh or impolite, and Trish was more concerned than anything.

Now, from the rear of the SUV after locking the office and setting the alarm, she is succumbing to tension and asks again and again who reported them missing.

'But, can I at least…?'

'…Mam.' The officer holds up a hand.

'You must have…'

'…Mam. As I said. Our orders were to escort you in to make a statement.'

'Yes, but you can't expect me to just…'

'…Mam! It'll be explained.'

Irritated, Trish pulls up the sleeves of her blazer, shifts in her seat and turns her eyes to the window.

The officers exchange looks.

She's stressed and beginning to feel something isn't right.

Barry lives alone, and Jyoti, like Trish, family-less, has a quartet of boyfriends she sees on a rotating basis. All convinced they're the one and only.

She dispenses with the idea that one of them reported her missing. Not this soon.

Watching the officers, she recognises the futility in pestering them any further. If they do know more, they're not going to share it, and if she pushes them any further, she'll only piss them off.

She tightens her hand into a fist and presses it into her chin as she watches the rural landscape surrounding their affordable office set in the hills 75 kilometres northeast of Seattle slip by.

What am I going to find out?

What could have happened to them?

I'm not ready to hear that they're…

METRO PRISON – DAY

Life is horror.

Someone has turned my life into a horror.

Why?

Trish's mind is spinning – working. Trying to make sense of it all. Trying to understand.

Barry and Jyoti have simply disappeared from the face of the Earth.

Her mind still holds the images of that first day. More

of an interview than an interrogation.

No accusations.

No charges.

Not even innuendos of guilt.

They'd taken her statement and cordially asked her to wait in a secure room while they processed her.

She had no idea what it meant.

Now, thirty-six days later, she sits on the bunk in her three metre by four metre room with a toilet and sink feeling tortured.

Solitary.

Bleak.

Lonely.

The shock that filled her that first day when they'd brought her clothes, a yellow prison jumpsuit, along with her first meal, and told her nothing, has turned into pernicious gloom.

No longer does she spend her days screaming through the door, or nights curled into a ball crying.

She has lost her impulse to harass the guards who bring her food.

She has given in and is barely able to keep from giving up.

There is just a remnant of hope.

Hope that this is some kind of mistake.

A mistake that someone will step in and fix.

She drops her face into her hands but decides not to cry.

TRISH'S CELL, MONTH SIX – DAY

Six months have passed.

Trish is on the floor with her knees up and hands behind her neck doing belly crunches.

She's counting aloud.

'45 – 46 – 47…'

The horror has resolved into a type of numb

acceptance.

Determined not to lose her strength or fall into another depression, she exercises constantly.

The thoughts of suicide have abated.

It is now defiance that drives her.

Something has told her that's what they, whoever they are, are hoping for. Are expecting.

And, as low as she'd gotten in that first six months, she isn't going to give it to them.

Without anyone to talk to, she's begun reciting poems, singing songs, and having philosophical or technical discussions with imaginary colleagues and professors. She is certain this will end and determined she will retain her verbal skills. And her ability to think.

She'd stopped pestering the guards after the fourth month for information. They are obviously under orders. Now, they simply bring her tray three times each day and once a week take her across the hall where she is allowed to shower and don a fresh set of prison clothes.

There is no happiness.

But the expectation that the door will open, and someone will come in and say this nightmare is over lingers.

'73 – 74 – 75…'

TRISH'S CELL, MONTH TEN

In the dark, Trish lies in her bunk staring at the ceiling.

Her face is blank.

After nine months, she has surrendered to complacency. Despondency is always just around the corner – waiting.

Life is four blank walls, push-ups, sit-ups, aerobic calisthenics and open debates with her scant furnishings.

Trish is now convinced she will die in a solitary cave never knowing why. Never knowing what happened to her partners.

Night after night she practises in her mind how not to feel. For her to exist, she has decided she must suppress her emotions.

The nights are no longer torture.

They are survival.

TRISH'S CELL, AFTER ONE YEAR – NIGHT

In the dark, well after midnight in late September, the armoured door to Trish Cordan's cell opens.

The movement startles her awake.

She sits – unafraid, but not understanding.

Twelve months and nine days have passed.

In those twelve months, the only contact she's had has been with her guards.

Delivering three meals each day.

Her weekly shower and change of clothes.

Not one ever engaging her in even trivial conversation.

There have been no other visitors.

Suddenly, with no warning, she is facing an unexpected guest.

But who?

And why now?

Why now when I have abandoned all hope?

A young woman moves into the light.

Trish gasps. 'My God!'

SEATTLE – OLD SECTION – DAY

The trip to the old section of the city, beyond the southern boundaries of the metropolis, took twenty minutes.

The odd jeep with a translucent shell, solar, amorphic silicon skin, pulls into the darkness beneath an elevated train platform.

The young woman in the back, seated next to a soldier, gazes at the desolation – the bleak remnants of a once modestly efficient city, and ponders.

The buildings are heavily graffitied or blackened. All openings are boarded.

In the middle of the street sit cars and trucks. Some are still smouldering. Many have been overturned.

The air smells of burnt rubber and sewage.

This is Hell.

An abandoned urban Hell.

To the north, through the cracks in the overhead railway network, she can see the metropolis. A world of pure science-fiction. Triangular, fully glazed, buildings, 100 – 150 – 200 storeys high sparkle as they turn on their foundations tracking the sun.

The sky hums with sleek, ultra-fast aerial transports slipping through transparent tubes like advanced hyper-loops – moving in and out of the rows of buildings.

Massive construction machines are everywhere pouring out new buildings – already finished. Some type of advanced, large-scale 3D construction printing.

The driver stops the jeep near a large vertical support.

The soldiers pull the girl out in the shade beneath the decaying platform.

'STOP!' She struggles and kicks. 'NO, GOD DAMN YOU!' She fights. 'NO!'

One has her arms the other her legs.

She's writhing like a snake trying to break free.

'Don't do this!'

They pull her to an abandoned storefront.

Her breathing quickens. Her eyes take in the other buildings. There is no one.

She continues fighting – kicking – scratching – biting – trying to break their grip.

The soldier at the front holds her – his hands are on her breasts – ripping at her clothes.

'Hands.' The soldier nods. 'Get her…'

'…I got her – I got her.'

The other, a savage smile on his face, releases her legs.

She kicks but chokes and stops when a savage hand

closes on her throat. She struggles to breathe watching the other unbuckle and drop his armoured pants.

His face is grotesque.

(CONT'D)

The elevated platform drenches the street below in gloomy darkness

Filthy, rust-coloured water drips from above.
The air is dense with mildew and rotting food.
A dog watches as the girl struggles.
The armoured men show no compassion.
Their intentions are understood.
Rape and murder.

OLD SEATTLE (CONT'D)

The rebuke is not planned. Is it?

Reflex?

The head butt to the soldier holding her jolts him. The follow-up elbow to the throat drops him to his knees gagging – gasping for air.

As the other struggles – pulling on his pants, the girl drops him with a kick to the groin then follows it with a sweeping kick to the side of his face.

He hits the ground hard and immediately reaches for his baton igniting it.

Not seeing the weapon, the girl moves quickly landing another kick, this time to the man's ribs.

She moves quickly and with skill.

But she is quiet.

Meticulous.

He heaves as he rolls over but is able to catch her on the left thigh with the baton.

Infrared, it burns like a red-hot poker from a fireplace.

'God damn you… you filthy…!'

She winces and falls to her knees – both hands holding

her thigh beneath her hip trying to close off the pain but says nothing.

Peripherally, she sees the soldier in the doorway regain his footing. Another baton is out – glowing bright red. This one coming right at her.

Dropping to a hand, she swings her free leg around cutting the man's legs out from beneath him. He falls with a thud. With him on his back, she has a moment to think and react.

She moves quickly, plants one foot on the man's wrist and drives the other into his jaw. He's down but still breathing. The baton falls from his hand. Obviously ignited by something in the mech-suit, it darkens,

She grabs it and limps over to the other who is still clutching at his ribs coughing up blood.

'Why?!'

She drops to her knees pressing the baton to his throat.

'Why me? Who sent you?'

The man sneers and shakes his head.

With both hands on the half metre long weapon, the girl snatches the man's consciousness with a blow to his head.

She stands – drops the baton and pulls her hands through her hair.

She peers down at the man.

'I didn't do anything God damn you!' She kicks him hard in the side. 'A year in that hole alone, and now you're trying to make me a *murderer*?'

She kicks him again. She feels wretched and ugly and violated and filled with hatred.

'Tell me, God damn you! Tell me what this is about.'

Tears streak her cheeks half in anger and half in rage as she continues kicking him.

'I think you can let that one go, babe.'

She spins.

And sets her eyes on a young man in a leather jacket and dark jeans with long brown hair leaning against a car lighting a cigarette.

This is Ethan Zane, a resistance fighter, a societal reject due to his innate disdain for authority. In his late twenties to early thirties standing in this blighted urban wilderness, he displays an almost surreal confidence.

(CONT'D)

'What do *you* want?'

'Nothing from you.' His voice is deep and gravelly.

Her look is contemptuous.

He pulls the cigarette from his lips and nods to his companions. A boy in his late teens with greasy hair and another, early twenties, gangly, sullen and dirty.

They move quickly from the car towards the fallen soldiers but stop as they reach the pavement. The men are still alive. Without a word, the younger boy pulls a gun from his pants and offers it to her. He points with his eyes to the soldiers. She takes it – examines it and looks down at the closest man. With two hands on the weapon, she points. Her hands shake. She tries and tries but is unable to carry it out.

The boy looks back to Ethan who nods.

The teen gently pulls the gun from her hands and quickly extinguishes both men. One shot to the head each. The girl turns away in disgust.

The two ragged young men begin stripping the soldiers down to their underwear.

'What are they doing?'

'What's it look like?' Ethan continues eyeing her. There's a subtle gleam of lust in his sun and wind-lined eyes.

'Their *combat gear*?'

'Mech-suits. Worth their weight in gold.'

The younger boy finishes, jams a baton into his belt, looks the girl in the eyes and tosses the mech-armour at her feet before returning to the car.

'What's this?'

'Consider it a gift. You don't take it, we will. But, uhm…' he looks at her ripped cotton prison wear, her shirt open and ripped exposing her breasts to her nipples, and grins. 'I think maybe… *you* should.' He smiles gazing down into her chest.

She stares him in the eyes – unable to read him seeing something more than cool confidence while she climbs into the light-weight acrylic armour.

Approval?

Acceptance?

'Who are you?' she asks while tightening the leggings.

'Jesus Christ, The Prophet, Cyrus the Great, Moses and Charlemagne babe. All rolled into one or take your pick. I'm righteous fucking salvation and damnation and One nation under God. And if I hadn't just seen you kick the shit out of those two soldiers looking for a little fun, I'd say shut the fuck up and get in the car. But…' he scans their bodies and snickers. 'As it is…' he climbs in through the window and starts the engine. 'I'll just say… need a lift?' He smiles with the cigarette bouncing between his lips.

She finishes latching the armour clasps across her chest and makes her way to the car.

'Yeah.'

INSIDE THE OLD POLICE CRUISER

She rounds the old cruiser and hops in.

The other two are in the back examining their bounty.

They make a quick turn towards the jeep and pull alongside.

The two in the back jump out and quickly strip what they can from the military vehicle loading it into the trunk.

'Aren't you going to take it?' The girl indicates the hi-tech jeep as the boys jump in.

'Nah,' says the driver who, though good looking, has

the appearance of someone with a lot of mileage on him. 'Piece of shit.' He nods to one of the guys in the back who lights a handmade fire bomb and launches it as they take off.

'Besides,' he says with his eyes on the road. 'We're not car thieves.'

The girl smiles and turns watching the jeep now gushing flames – the amorphic silicon shell melting.

The old, modified police cruiser with a cracked windshield speeds through the darkened streets beneath the dead shell of the elevated train.

She watches the gutted, fire blackened buildings, the emaciated remains of a once pristine boulevard, flash by.

Cars, some still smouldering, litter the streets and the driver seems unconcerned while weaving in and out at a savage pace.

'Ethan.' He says – lighting another cigarette.

She looks to the back.

'That's Derek.' The greasy haired teen nods. 'And the quiet one's Leo. Leo don't talk much. Don't talk at all come to think of it.'

'Why not?' She turns and glances at the remote young man staring down into a ceramic device he'd taken from the jeep.

'Don't know. Never asked him.' He grins. 'How bout you? What got you locked up in our happy little community?'

She shrugs and looks forward. 'I'm Trish. Trisha Cordan.'

It's as if she'd said she were a live hand grenade.

Ethan hits the brakes – his casual expression suddenly changed. The car screeches to a stop throwing Trish nearly through the windshield.

With the car stopped at a desolate intersection, Ethan turns – reaches a hand over and grabs her by the throat.

'Don't shit me! I'll throw you right out of the fucking car.' His face is fierce. '*Who are you?*'

Trish tries swallowing. His grip is tight.

'Trisha. I'm Trisha Cordan. And I don't have a God damn clue why they locked me up.'

He looks to the back – to his companions, withdraws his hand and takes a breath. His eyes dart. He holds the wheel, drops his head to his hands then turns facing her.

'What you did for a living before this?'

'*Before what?*' She appears to have no idea of what he's referring to, or what triggered his response.

He nods towards the metropolis in the distance. His words are anxious – rushed and accusatory. 'That! Before any of it?! Your job! What was your job?!'

She still appears confused – her voice quick and nervous. 'Computers. I had my own software company. We did databases for businesses. Here and overseas.'

He holds his mouth.

'What?' She swallows. '*What is it?*' she turns to the boy in the back. His expression is dark.

'*What?*'

Ethan starts the car.

She grabs his arm. '*Tell me!*'

He swings the car around. 'You're myth babe. Fable. And there's someone northwest of Pantheon who needs to see you.'

'*Pantheon?*' Her eyes widen.

'Yeah.' He steps on the gas and swerves between two overturned cars – gives her a sideways look. 'And if you are who you say you are… I'll bet you've heard *that* term before.'

She gasps, sinks back into the seat and watches as the car picks up speed and the silver, white and glass metropolis grows closer.

METRO SECURITY CENTRE – DAY

The ultra-modern, austere room is electric.

Men and women in white, Pantheon security operators,

move in and out of suspended transparent screens.

All movement – everyone in the western city state is monitored from this massive theatre.

Control and order are key components to the city's stability.

The air hums with excitement.

Trish Cordan has been found.

Hidden away in a rural prison by someone. For her safety?

Silver-white light filters down from the ceiling making the room surreal.

Conversations overlap.

The professional manner of the operators masks a deeper concern.

Trish Cordan has killed the soldiers sent by the president before her abduction from the presidential estate to remove her as a threat to Pantheon.

The order is to find her.

The order supersedes all others.

THE SECURITY CENTRE (CONT'D)

'Is she still alone?'

General Malik, a stern, bald man of fifty walks into the security centre with Colonel Matthews at his heels.

'Someone picked her up shortly after she…'

'…*Someone?*' The general turns. A questioning stare – a weighted, ugly pause.

The colonel grasps his consternation.

There is no one in the old sector but terrorists, derelicts, felons and those without means – the infirm. Those offering no benefit to society. Allowed to wither and die… of *natural* causes.

Society has been redesigned with rules. The structure is strict. No one, not even the military or police are allowed to use lethal force accept in self-defence.

It is efficient and accepted.

Crime within the metropolis is unknown. Rules are followed without question. There is order.

The general turns into a narrow row of suspended screens and walks.

He approaches a young female technician.

'Bring up the old section to the south. Twenty-four.'

The girl's expression is strange. What?

She touches something on her studded glove and holds it to the expansive glass panel. The wire frame outline of a city grows.

She turns her hand and the scene zooms to rows of abandoned buildings. Section 24. Why that section?

'How many?'

'Total?' he nods. With the operator's next adjustment, textual data begins streaming down the left side of the panel. '23 018.' She turns her eyes to the military official.

'Eliminate the known derelicts, children under twelve, and the infirm.'

The outline on the screen changes to magenta.

More textual data streams.

Names – sex – alphanumeric identifiers – other parameters: Age – Weight – Arrest records – Sexual preference – Physical defects.

'One hundred ninety-three.' She turns and faces him. 'But the number is inaccurate.'

'Why?'

She returns to the screen – the micro pinpoints of light moving – disappearing – others appearing.

'Because the number continually changes.'

The general ponders this with a hand stroking his chin – aware the terrorist element, as difficult as it is to imagine, has gained technology. At least the technology to hide from the world-wide communications and surveillance network.

What other technologies they may have amassed is, for the moment, speculation.

He turns to Colonel Matthews. 'Your efforts to deal

with this situation effectively have been a demonstration of *your* weakness. And of ours.'

The colonel appears stung. 'I lose good men every time we go in looking for someone. Nine last week. Twelve the week before. A month ago we lost...'

The general holds up a stiff hand silencing him.

'I'm uninterested in your statistics, Colonel Matthews.' He walks to the end of the aisle. 'Return to your base colonel. You're relieved.'

'But, sir. If I can...'

'...Must I say it again?'

'No sir, I just...'

'...I will now take full command of eradicating this group and finding Trisha Cordan.'

'And of the president? Will you also...?'

'...Of course. Her safe return is my top concern.'

The colonel stands and watches as the general leaves. He turns to the operator. Her expression is blank and offers him nothing.

THE JORLAN JONES ESTATE – DAY

The vast room is dark and cluttered.

A converted storeroom in the back of an Asian restaurant in a run-down area in the old city once called China Town.

In the darkness, with only a hazy yellow light filtering in through a strip of curtained windows along the ceiling, Trish wanders trying to draw a picture of this Jorlan. The man Ethan said would answer her questions.

She stops at a large antique dining table laden with ancient, cloth-bound books. They are dust covered and yellowed.

Her eyes scan. The room is filled with similar antiques. Tables, chairs, a dining hutch. An old Jukebox. Magnificent portraits along the walls. Museum pieces. Archaic astronomical tools: Astrolabes – Orreries.

She moves to a row of walnut stained shelves. Helmets with electronic visors. Weapons. Batons like the one strapped to her leg. Mech armour. Conventional weapons: handguns, rifles, grenades.

She pulls from the shelf a short pump-action shotgun. Police issue. She studies it.

'Ever use one?'

The voice is mannered, soft and articulate.

She decides not to turn.

'No.' She speaks casually and continues studying the weapon. 'I hate it.'

She returns it to the shelf and turns to the young man in a light green suit over a white silk shirt seated in a throne-like chair with his hands together in front of him – his fingers interwoven.

This is Jorlan Jones. A legendary terrorist thought by most Pantheon residents, and many officials, not to exist. He's blonde, with piercing green eyes, trim and appears deeply contemplative. Almost… brooding.

He's a thinker who chooses knowledge over emotion and sees no loss in the trade.

Trish edges closer trying to get a better look at his face.

He eyes her as she moves into the light.

'I knew we would one day have this meeting.'

He's articulate, deeply ethereal, and soft spoken with a slight accent that Trish identifies as English.

She moves closer. 'You did?'

'Yes.' He gazes down at an elaborate chess board set in front of him on a raised metal and glass pedestal. 'I've always wondered what my first question to you would be.'

She stops where the tiles meet a massive oriental rug.

'Did you ever reach a conclusion?'

She glides slowly into a garish, upholstered armchair facing him.

'I did.'

She waits. He seems odd to her. Hardly what she was expecting. He's like a young executive. Blonde, Handsome.

A terrorist leader? She's finding it difficult to imagine.

'What did you decide?'

He tilts his head.

'Why?' The air holds the question in a tense grip. 'Though, I do recognise how trite that may sound. But it occurred to me one day while sitting in my office, watching the machines pouring out a modern city after levelling much of the old one, that… you were either a supreme visionary, a delusional idealist or a daft fool. And regardless which of the three you turned out to be, I continued to land on that same question. Why?' He raises his eyes to hers. 'Why did you do it?'

She feels a sudden coldness that is both inside and outside of her.

Reasons.

There were many.

All rational.

Logical.

She wants to respond but is unnerved by this man. This resistance leader who has been able to hide from the authorities worldwide. A man who has maintained his control over terrorists who still pose a threat to the security of the people of Pantheon and other city-states across the globe.

A man who still has the militaries, on four continents, with all their resources baffled.

She needs to know more.

She glances down at the chess table and thinks.

And chooses to remain quiet.

'Do you play?' He leans forward – his eyes are on the chessboard.

'I did. My father taught me when I was…'

He looks up. His stare is questioning. It's as if… as if he knows something. Or perhaps *everything* about her.

'I was little.'

'Do you remember the rules?'

She squints. 'Yes.'

He reaches out and begins resetting the board.

When finished, he again weaves his fingers together and places them beneath his chin.

'I'm Jorlan. Shall we?'

HOURS LATER

Over the next two hours, Jorlan and Trish play and talk. Though the chess game is the focus, the real game is being played out in their probing questions.

Each is a mystery to the other, and neither feels certain of where this meeting will take them.

Trish finds Jorlan an enigma. And masterful at remaining one, answering every question she poses with one of his own.

She feels, at the end of the two hours, she knows as little about him as she did when she'd sat down.

Masterfully evasive?

Undoubtedly.

During their first game, she asks him how long he's been the leader of this resistance, or rebellion. Or whatever they're calling it. It seems to her an obvious question.

He returns with: 'in your estimation, is one considered rebellious because they defy authority, or simply because they question it?'

She ponders the question but offers no response.

He seems to know much about her, which she derives from his reactions to her describing her work at SenTEK up until the moment of her detainment and subsequent imprisonment.

This unnerves her, and she wonders how much more he knows.

'I'm afraid that's checkmate again, Trish.'

She drops her King.

He leans forward – his eyes keen and penetrating.

'You've been told, I understand, our president, your creation, who shared her domination scheme with the world – has reconstructed herself as Tess Cordan. Made herself an organic entity. Human.' He pauses. 'In your image.'

'Yes.'

His eyes are suddenly on fire.

'And you know it was PANTHEON that gave her and the others, around the world, that ability.'

'Yes. But I had no idea when I gave it to her what her intentions were. What she was planning to do with it.'

Trish tries anticipating where he's going with this line of questioning.

His eyes, those trenchant eyes, are staring through her. She feels certain there is nothing she can conceal from him. Nor, for some reason, does she want to. This... *feeling* disturbs her.

She'd brought something from the past into the future and handed it to the consummate strategist who'd in turn shared it with the world. The world of intelligent machines. Machines that proceeded to make themselves real and remake the world in a manner that most pleased them. A world based on logic, efficiency and order.

An ideal environment for them to flourish and reign supreme. But not as computers or robots. With PANTHEON, a language that could rearrange matter at the elemental level, they could live. They'd made themselves real. They'd made themselves human.

But better than human, for they'd improved themselves. Their brains would still be supercomputer fast and could still rearrange matter. Man had made machines and the machines, desirous of what man had, had made themselves man. It was an elaborate irony. An evolutionary circle no one had even hypothesised.

She awaits the final question.

The one she knows he will ask.

The one no one has *ever* asked.

The one she covets.

The demon she has locked away.

'Trisha.' He brings his eyes up to hers. They freeze her. 'Who is TESS?'

She feels compressed and breathless and closes her eyes. It's finally time to tell someone the truth.

THE LAKE

The sun climbs high above the trees.

The water glistens.

The lake is now a mirror-like reflection of the old-growth trees encircling it.

The girl in the shorts stands.

She runs to the end of the pier.

Precocious – more adventurous, she taunts her timid sister.

'Bet I can swim across.' She laughs.

The girl in the sundress ignores her.

She's just trying to scare me, she thinks.

The girl edges out onto her toes.

'I'll do it,' she threatens.

'Stop or I'll tell,' says the girl dropping her flowers.

The girl in the shorts smiles.

But the smile goes away as she loses her balance and falls.

The girl in the sundress climbs to her feet and runs to the end.

She freezes.

Neither girl can swim.

'Help me Trisha.'

Trisha turns towards the house.

She tries to yell, but no words come out.

She returns her eyes to the lake and falls to her knees. She tries reaching.

Tess is frantic and splashing.

She's drifted too far.

'TRISHA!'

'TESSY!'

She reaches again and almost follows her in.

Trish is frozen – sobbing.

Tears flood her eyes. She feels and is helpless.

She screams, but it is no use.

In another minute, her twin sister Tess is at the bottom of the lake.

Trisha Cordan is screaming, crying, inconsolable, calling.

'TESSY! TESSY! COME BACK! TESSY…!' She turns to the house. 'MOMMY! DADDY! COME… HURRY!'

But there is no answer.

No one hears.

She tries again.

'MOMMY! DADDY! TESSY IS IN THE LAKE!'

The house is far and the girl's call is again unanswered.

The lake is quiet now, and the water is again a placid mirror.

When she returns to the house, Trisha Cordan is an only child.

THE JORLAN JONES ESTATE (CONT'D)

'Have you ever heard of the Gloucester syndrome?'

'No.'

Jorlan leans close. 'People have been designing companions since the beginning of AI research. Many just for the science but others to fill a void. The loss of a loved one. Or simply to conquer loneliness. With so much of themselves programmed into an artificial entity, and with constant contact, a programmer can lose touch with reality. Actually change places with the artificial companion.'

Trish turns sideways in the wide-winged armchair and drapes her legs over the side.

She feels Jorlan studying her. She is examining his choice of words and wonders why he's probing her.

'You're crying.'

She wipes her eyes on her sleeve. 'Does that surprise you?'

'No. All intelligent beings, real or artificial, possess the ability to feel and display emotion. Aristotle described it as a requirement in the human species. Called it a catharsis.'

'What are you saying?'

'That you're suffering, and you're trying to release your inner torment.'

He stands, walks to her and holds out a hand. 'Come.' She takes his hand and holds it. 'I'd like to show you my collections.'

She hesitates.

Jorlan gives her a slight reassuring smile. 'Come. The past holds answers. Answers for all of us.'

She climbs from the chair.

DINING ROOM, JONES ESTATE – NIGHT

Ethan sits with Jorlan at a large round table eating noodles with chopsticks.

Light, from magnificent Chinese and Japanese chandeliers, pours down on this traditionally decorated, lavish dining room.

Ornate museum statues: Buddhas – Bodhisattvas – Shiva – Vishnu – Temple guardians and Lions are everywhere ringing the three large and six smaller tables.

The walls, fronted in seamless glass panels, hold Tang and Ming dynasty Chinese paintings – many with small museum placards stating the description and date.

One realises immediately, this is much more than an estate. This is a full urban block of interconnected restaurants, shops and hotels holding incalculable treasure.

'You torched the jeep?'

Ethan nods his head but continues eating. 'Didn't see any reason to take it.'

They wait while Mrs Huifen, a dignified old Chinese woman, serves them tea.

'Will there be anything else, Mr Jorlan Sir?'

He tilts his head to her with a slight, very proper smile. 'No, Mrs Huifen.' Jorlan looks to Ethan who shrugs.

'I'm good. This is great. I'm eating here every day from now on.'

Mrs Huifen bows and grumbles as she turns to the kitchen. 'Savages.'

Ethan nearly chokes on his tea.

He looks to Jorlan who sustains a soft grin with a hand to his mouth.

'Well. Any day now I'm expecting her to re-evaluate her position on what we do for a living.'

They laugh more.

'The location recorder?'

Ethan smiles, wipes his mouth and pulls a small ceramic device from his jacket pocket. Hands it to Jorlan who studies it. 'Leo snagged it from the jeep after we picked her up. Just before we sent it into the afterlife.'

Ethan returns to his noodles but keeps his eyes on Jorlan who is studying the complex device. 'Why d'you want that?'

'This holds a recording of everything ever said in that jeep. It also maintains a record of everywhere it's been.'

'Yeah? So, what are you going to do with it?'

'I'll download this after we finish here. Then… then I have a little task for you.' He looks him in the eyes. 'A little journey I'd like you and your boys to take.'

Jorlan pockets the device and stands.

'Stay here tonight. Grab vacant rooms in the hotel. I'd like you, Leo and Derek to leave in the morning.'

Ethan continues eating but says nothing as Jorlan turns to leave. But before taking a step, he's struck with an afterthought.

'Odd, don't you think?'

'Hmm?'

'That the soldiers decided to kill her there? In one of our neighbourhoods?'

From Ethan's look, one gathers he does not see this as strange. 'Guess they wanted to plant it on us.'

From *Jorlan's* look, he is unconvinced.

'I question the logic in that strategy. Trish Cordan has been portrayed by Pantheon as a threat. This would make her valuable to the terrorists.' He shrugs. 'Us. A better strategy, from their perspective, exists.'

He does not appear ready to share more of his scepticism.

'I think they just wanted to do her and dump it on us.'

Jorlan's face is that of a supreme strategist. He holds his scepticism.

'Perhaps.'

Jorlan leaves Ethan alone with his noodles and sushi. Even Ethan, a long-trusted soldier in this resistance, has difficulty reading him, yet... he does not look inconvenienced by this. He is infinitely more interested in his noodles and manipulating his chop sticks.

JORLAN'S ESTATE – NIGHT

Trish spends the next week with Jorlan dining, playing chess, discussing the technology and philosophy of the new order and exploring his maze of interconnected restaurants, hotels, and gift shops. The elaborate domain he's created in the middle of an urban district.

From the outside – it looks nothing. Neglected turn-of-the-century buildings crammed together facing a narrow street set beneath the China Town elevated rail platform. The inside is rich and filled with fabulous art and antiques and books and rare artefacts. Remnants of the old world. Refuse to the new one.

JORLAN'S URBAN GALLERIES – NIGHT

'It's more of a museum than a base of operations.'

After another night of eating in one of the smaller

dining rooms, talking until late while playing chess, Trish follows Jorlan down a long corridor through the galleries. Exhibit rooms fronted with glass. Modern. Out of place. It resembles the old world's most elaborate museum.

'It's amazing.'

She walks slowly in a sexy black dress with spaghetti straps watching him – wondering how he's made this incredibly extravagant museum inside these decaying buildings and has managed, *is* managing, to avoid the search scans of the authorities.

He stops at a junction and turns.

'You've not asked me the question I posed you the day you arrived. When we first met.' His eyes canvass the galleries then land on hers.

'What question?' He stares. She feels a sudden discomfort. It's as if he's looking into her. 'I don't remember, Jorlan.'

His expression is unreadable.

Again her mind works trying to analyse him – his feelings about her.

What are you thinking?

Trish replays the day she'd arrived with meticulous accuracy. But with his cold eyes staring into her, unnerving her, her memories are blurred.

Jorlan taps a thumb to his upper lip and appears pensive. Without a word, he turns away from her and passes out of the gallery through a metal door.

Trish leans her backside on the glass and slides to the floor frustrated.

She gazes into a gallery on the other side of the corridor. A baby grand piano. 19th century. An antique sofa with walnut legs.

Portraits in elaborate gold frames. Rembrandt, Cezanne Raphael, Rubens.

She closes her eyes.

'Why?'

Irritated with herself, she stands and slams a hand into

the glass.

She holds her reddened palm to her face.

'Why?!'

ETHAN'S POLICE CRUISER – NIGHT

In armoured leather mech-pants, boots and a heavy brown shirt, Trish sits opposite Ethan as they speed through the deserted streets of the old city's west side.

Both are heavily armed with police batons and revolvers.

Ethan has a short Bull-Pup shotgun strapped to his leg.

They're driving fast – weaving between burnt cars and large garbage drums. Many are glowing and billowing smoke.

The air is tense.

One can look at Ethan's typically confident face and know there is danger, even for them, in this section of the city.

Men and women, derelicts, scurry out of their way as they pass. Many yell obscenities. Some hurl bottles and cans. Tish holds the revolver in her lap.

Ethan catches the look on her face.

She finds the gun repellent.

Her reaction is expected.

'Who is this guy we're supposed to see?'

Trish places a foot on the dash.

'Someone important to Jorlan. He asked me to give him that.' He nods to the rear seat to a thin laptop sleeve.

'What's in it?'

'Don't know. It's none of *my* business.' He lights a cigarette. 'That's one thing I've never been burdened with.'

'What?'

'Curiosity.'

He pulls on the cigarette and blows a stream of smoke out the window.

'Why did he want me with you?'

He glances at her peripherally.

'Don't know that one either.' He smiles. 'Maybe he thought you were getting bored back at the palace.'

She chuckles as Ethan pulls the car into an alley behind a row of commercial high rises.

It's dark.

There is one dim light stuck to the loading dock of a building at the far end and a dimmer one hanging from a pole in the middle.

He turns off the engine and leans back. 'Now we wait.'

'Can I ask you something?'

'I'd say no, but I'm quite sure you'll ask anyway, so…' He smiles and faces her. '…have at it.'

'How does Jorlan get the art pieces and statues?'

'That's strike three babe. Maybe he buys the shit. Who the fuck knows. Who the fuck cares? Worthless shit if you ask me.'

'You don't ever see it brought in?'

'You know…'

He reaches an arm over the seat and grabs the sleeve then hands it out the window to a wiry man of forty in a sleeveless vest who appears from the shadows. His arms are fully tattooed.

No words are exchanged.

Ethan simply nods as the fellow takes it and watches him scamper back into the building through the rear utility door.

Ethan starts the car, turns and faces her.

'There were guys who found a way to get rich during the depression. There were even guys who made money during the plagues in Europe selling soap.' He scratches his head. 'I kind of think Jorlan is one of those guys.

'Drop him naked in a fuckin forest and he'd find a way to drive out in a Ferrari wearin a silk suit.'

They laugh as Ethan shifts and moves the car ahead into the darkened alley. But stops when he sees a quartet of men blocking the opening.

The men are ragged and armed. One cocks a pump-action shotgun.

They wait.

'Shit.'

'Who are they?'

Jorlan scans the alley – shifts into reverse and begins backing into the darkness trying to see out the cracked rear window.

'Demons from the underworld, babe. Darkness that makes the night seem bright.'

The beat-up police cruiser rams a row of metal drums pushing them into the alley.

'God damn it!'

Ethan pulls forward – straightens the car and again starts backing but stops.

The alley behind them is blocked with grey metal dumpsters. More men with weapons stand behind and between them. This is a well-planned trap.

He looks ahead then turns his gaze to the revolver in Trish's lap.

She follows his eyes – knows the question before he releases it.

She holds her breath.

'Will you use that?'

She nods. He can feel her tension.

'I know you can… will you?'

She grabs it, breathes and nods.

He pulls a similar gun from his pocket and revs the engine.

The air is bleeding tension.

'Then put that fucking thing out the window and start pulling the trigger and don't stop until I tell you.'

He drops the car into gear, puts his gun out the window and together they fly down the alley, slamming into dumpsters and barrels burning the air with .45 calibre automatics.

ETHAN'S CRUISER (CONT'D)

Once through the men and back out onto the boulevard, with a pulverised windshield – most of it small glass kernels in their laps, Ethan grabs Trish's hand and stops her from firing.

He's laughing as he takes the gun from her and drops it back into her lap.

She opens her eyes. Her face is pure jubilation.

'I did it!'

She turns to him – her eyes glow with the excitement of a child. 'I did it, Ethan! I did it!'

'You did.' He nods, smiles, down shifts and screeches around an overturned bus. 'You didn't hit a God damn thing, but you definitely get an A for effort.'

They continue laughing as Ethan makes a series of quick turns planting them on a northbound boulevard back towards China Town.

The road is dark, and the car is now cool with the wind rushing in unimpeded.

Trish clears away some broken glass from the dash and from their clothes then sits back in the seat.

Her mind works as she looks down at the gun in her lap.

Her face is suddenly changed.

'Was this the real reason Jorlan wanted me with you?' She doesn't face him – keeps her eyes on the gun. Her respect for Jorlan as the consummate strategist grows. 'To see if I could use this?'

The car suddenly feels cold. Was it?

'Funny guy, Jorlan. As long as I've known him, I still don't have a clue why he does things. That's why there's never been a problem between us.'

'Why?'

'Because I'm not interested in knowing why he does things. So…' He faces her. 'So I never lose sleep thinkin about it and he never feels the need to tell me.'

JORLAN'S ESTATE – DAY

Trish is walking alone through the long rows of interconnected museum like galleries. She drags her fingers along the glass as she passes from one to the next.

Her face holds a soft smile. She's different. There's a calmness about her. Even her clothes have changed.

She's in dark jeans and a deep teal shirt and her hair is cut short to her head.

The transformation in the week following her excursion with Ethan is remarkable. It's as if she's erased six years and would now look comfortable strutting across a university campus.

At the junction, she turns through the main dining room and walks through the kitchen to the central courtyard.

She walks to the glass and stops with her fingertips stroking the slightly tinted panes. The estate is quiet. She waits and watches feeling calm and at home.

In the courtyard, amongst the exotic trees, fountains and flowers, stands Jorlan polishing a large stone Buddha.

In green dress pants and a soft white shirt with his sleeves rolled, his hands glide, pulling a tan chamois over the magnificent statue.

Drawn to him – to being *here* with him in his pristine urban wonderland, Trish finally steps through the glass door and follows the stone path over a small bridge to Jorlan and the Buddha.

'Is it new?'

'Hardly.' He regards her but continues polishing. 'Qing Dynasty. 17th century.'

She's learning him and is unoffended and untouched by his flippant remark. He knew her question.

She circles it.

She's trying, struggling to understand his preoccupation with his relics.

Old, but eternal.

Immortal.

She wants more each day to be a part of him. To see and feel his world through his eyes.

She feels a desire she's never felt. To be mated. To be his. And have him share his love with her.

But he is preoccupied as she approaches, and she again feels rejected.

Again, frustrated, she wants to lash out. To say notice me! Hold me! Love me, God damn you! Her arms clench watching him. Her face reddens.

She feels the urge to strike him.

He continues polishing his statue oblivious to her.

'Come.'

She's startled from her anger.

It's Mrs Huifen. She saw her from the kitchen and has come to her rescue.

'You help me in kitchen today.' She gives her a warm smile. An expression she didn't know the old woman owned.

She takes her by the hand – pulls her gracefully.

'We make fried shrimp in ultimate secret sauce no one in whole world knows but me.'

Smiling and warm, Trish allows the old woman to pull her back into the kitchen.

She gives only a fleeting glance at Jorlan as she closes the door.

Her anguish is gone.

Mrs Huifen is keen and perceptive.

Trisha decides to love her.

THEATRE, JORLAN'S ESTATE – DAY

'How much of PANTHEON do you remember?'

Jorlan and Trish are standing in the centre aisle of a video theatre at the south end of his estate. It has a massive 20-metre-wide by four-metre-high curved screen. Thirty plush chairs that look like they came from a 20th century concert hall sit in even rows in the centre. The walls are hung with deep maroon drapes and the cut-glass chandeliers are brilliant and ornate.

'Some. Why?'

'Can you picture the code in your mind?'

'I think so.'

He pulls a military baton from behind him. His swift movement startles her.

'Imagine this glowing.' She nods. 'If I swing it and strike you on the neck… you'll die.' He looks her hard in the eyes. 'Make it go away Trisha.'

Jorlan raises the baton and quickly brings it down but holds the downward thrust when he sees her close her eyes waiting patiently for him to strike her.

He squints, and, as she reopens her eyes, she sees puzzlement rather than the usual confidence in his face. Something has happened, and she is now convinced of his suspicion.

He's testing her.

Resolve?

Commitment?

Or…

She takes his hand and looks at him with a quiet question in her soft, affectionate eyes.

'Do you like me?'

Jorlan brings a finger to his lips. He is quietly contemplative.

'Is it important to you?'

'I've never allowed anyone to like me. And if they tried, I found ways to make them stop.'

He holds her chin.

'That's an interesting formula.'

'I'll ask again. Do you like me?'

Jorlan leans in and kisses her lips, pulls away and smiles. 'If I said no, you would ask me why. And I would then deflect by telling you how attractive I find you. And you would accept the compliment yet be dissatisfied.

'However, if I told you yes, you would feel satisfied but concerned that I was simply trying to spare you the feelings of rejection.'

Trish gives him a curious look.

'Can I ask you another question? One less likely to elicit a think four moves ahead type answer?'

Jorlan smiles and lightens.

Trish feels certain she has now received the answer to her question.

'Of course.'

'Why?'

He appears confused but also intrigued. 'Why what?'

She smiles and kisses his cheek.

Her smile is a patronising one.

'I promised Mrs Huifen I would help her move books in her unit. Will we play chess again tonight?'

He strokes his lip and studies her.

She kisses him again, smiles and turns making her way from the theatre.

JORLAN'S MAIN ROOM – DAY

Trish enters the large, cluttered room where she first met with Jorlan. It is early, just seven, and he is again seated in his large throne-like chair dressed in a medium blue suit and cream-white shirt.

There are others.

All are seated facing him. Ethan, who gives her a nod and a smile as she wanders through the antiques, the young boy with stringy hair she remembers from the day she fought with the soldiers, and the one named Leo who never speaks. There are three others she's never met.

They've been talking. From their expressions, it is obvious to her it was about something important.

She sits in an armchair to the left of Jorlan.

He regards her. 'I asked for you to join us.'

'Mrs Huifen woke me. She said you were waiting in

your den.'

Jorlan, hardly the expressive type, smiles. 'Did she call it that?'

Trish is warmed by the feeling that she can now amuse him almost at will. She's getting closer to him and feels he is beginning to trust her.

She assumes trust in their world is something which must be earned. She's adapting. This is not the world of SenTEK. Of Barry and Jyoti. This is a war where the rules of engagement are skewed.

'She did.' She chuckles. 'With a little derision in her voice.'

Jorlan laughs and turns to the others.

'I'm glad you're all more committed to this than our wonderful Mrs Huifen.'

They add their laughter to his.

'Trisha…' Jorlan leans forward with his elbows planted on his knees. He is now severe. 'There's a General Malik in Patheon. He's the closest adviser to your sister. He's the top military man. It appears she placed him in charge of security, and… of finding you prior to her abduction. We assume, by this, he was *not* the one who ordered your imprisonment, or more recently, your murder.'

Trish takes a moment to think.

'Perhaps he replaced the one who had?'

Jorlan's eyes leave hers then return.

'Can you think of a way we can find out for sure?'

Trisha's eyes dart to the others. She is torn again, silently questioning his motivation for asking her.

Is the constant questioning truly to test her resolve?

Is there no end to satisfying his suspicions about her?

She is still suffering – unable to read him.

'Simple.' Her answer comes off as abrupt and confident. 'Abduct him and ask him.'

Her response elicits laughter. From Ethan, mostly, who tilts his head back.

Except for Jorlan, who continues staring while

sweeping his bottom lip with a single finger, they all find her suggestion amusing.

'And I should be the one to do it.'

This quiets them as they now assume she is serious.

Jorlan studies her while stroking his chin.

'Why you?'

'Three reasons. I caused this. It needs to be done. And if *I* do it, you'll no longer mistrust me.'

Jorlan continues to stare.

She has yet again puzzled him. He stands.

'Tomorrow morning. The general leaves his residence at 07:00. Never a minute later. He'll be on the steps of the presidential estate and most vulnerable at 07:30.' He casts his eyes on Ethan. 'She'll need a firearm. An untraceable one. Ceramic. One that won't be picked up by the city's EM scan.'

Ethan nods. 'I'll take care of it.'

'See me later in my suite. We'll discuss the details. The route you'll take once you have the general in the car. Where you'll go from there.'

Ethan looks to Trish who has her eyes locked on Jorlan who is, as always when conducting business, deeply contemplative. He is like a man whose mind never rests. Always calculating. Always pouring over a problem looking at it from multiple angles.

He looks at Trish – his eyes are sharp and penetrating.

'He'll recognise you. Even with your hair changed. This will be advantageous as his alarm will grant you the time you'll need to act.'

Trish stares him in the eyes.

'You mean he'll recognise me as Tess.'

'Of course. She did make herself in your image. Or that of your twin sister.'

She squints and watches as he slowly walks from the room.

(CONT'D)

Ethan stands.

'Well babe. We're off to Oz in the morning. Get your sleep and don't forget your ruby slippers.'

He makes a move for the door.

'Ethan?'

'Yeah.' He stops and turns.

'Please, don't be evasive with me. Not like you have been in the past. What can you tell me about Jorlan?'

'I'm not… you know…'

'…Please?'

He sighs, drops back into his chair and lights a cigarette. She has persuaded him. 'Not much. He was an industrial engineer or something on the east coast. Tiranon. Old New York City.'

This has obviously startled her.

'You mean, he wasn't slated for submission like the rest of you?'

He smiles. 'Where d'you pick that term up?'

'I don't know.' She appears nervous. 'Probably one of the attendants or the other guys coming in and out of here when you're not around.' She shrugs. 'Maybe Mrs Huifen.'

He chuckles and shakes his head. 'Nah. Not Jorlan. He was an insider. You see the way he dresses. One day, as I understand it, he was looking out of his office, watching them scrape our world off the map to make way for theirs, and… I don't know. Guess he kind of liked the way things were. Flawed, smutty, corrupt. Guess it held some appeal for him. Some people are funny that way. They'd rather accept something broke and familiar than something new and untested. He left that day and went… I don't know. Underground, I guess. Then… he ended up here.'

'Hmm.' Scepticism crosses her face.

He watches her.

'What do you honestly think he's going to do with all this stuff? The antiques? The art? Everything else?'

'I've told you. I don't know. Maybe he sees things going back to the way they were someday. Maybe he plans to open his own museum. Who knows? He seems to like you. Why don't you ask him?'

'Does he have someone? You know… Like a…?'

'…What. *A wife? Girlfriend?*'

She nods.

'Not that I know of. Why? You volunteering for the position?'

She appears far away in thought. 'Just curious.'

'Well.' He stands – takes a deep drag on his cigarette and blows the smoke at the ceiling. He then drops his eyes to hers. 'Don't ponder it too long. We got a busy day tomorrow.'

'Thanks, Ethan.'

'Anytime.'

He nods, smiles and leaves.

TRISH'S ROOM – NIGHT

It is after 8PM when a knock sounds at Trish's door.

'Jorlan.'

'Can I come in?'

'Of course.'

Trish is startled but hides it well. She's been playing chess against the computer at a desk in the corner of her room on the second floor of the hotel.

She feels stimulated when she catches his eyes as she turns in her silk night shirt which just touches the top of her bikini panties. It's warm. The pants she's left on the bathroom door.

Jorlan is, as always, well-dressed in a light grey suit and charcoal shirt. With his blonde hair and wide blue eyes, she finds him increasingly attractive.

'I picked these out for you for tomorrow.'

He hands her a tan pleated skirt, soft rayon shirt, high heels, and a light-coloured blazer.

'They should fit.'

Trish takes the clothes over her arm.

'Will you stay for a while?' Though trying not to, her look is unmistakably seductive.

He takes in a deep breath and clears his throat. 'I will.' She smiles and steps away from the door. He shakes his head – but just gently. 'But not tonight.'

She feels foolish and rejected.

She was literally offering herself to him.

It frustrates her.

'Are you winning, Trisha?'

He stares her in the eyes. She freezes. Her heart races.

'What do you mean?'

He nods over her shoulder to the computer.

She breathes, chuckles and turns. 'Oh. That. Occasionally. Not very often. But, I'm in the middle of a good game now.'

He gives her a soft smile. 'Don't give up.' He moves to the door. 'You're very talented. I believe you're someone who will succeed at anything you put your mind to.'

He steps out into the hall and pulls the door shut behind him.

Trish closes her eyes and pulls the clothes to her breast.

She is again frustrated.

Frustrated, rejected and angered.

TRISH'S ROOM – NIGHT

Long after Jorlan has left, with the room dark, Trish is startled awake by a dream.

She sits

The room is cold.

Biting cold.

The door opens.

'Mrs Huifen. Is there something wrong?'

'No heat tonight. Men work on it now.' She has a light-yellow duvet and begins covering her. When finished, she sits on the edge of the bed and motherly strokes Trish's head. Trish lies back.

'I was dreaming an awful dream.'

'Shh.' She touches her cheek with the back of her fingers. 'Cold bring bad dreams. Warmth chase them away.'

She looks the kind old woman in the eyes.

For a moment they stare.

The room seems to hold their thoughts.

'Why can't I get him to love me?'

'Shh. Mr Jorlan is a complicated man. He is the silence in the world. You are the moment that fell into his silence. But silence is not fast to accept change.' She nods. 'He just need more time.'

She smooths a hand through her boyish hair and smiles.

'I do good job, yes?'

Trish hugs her.

'Will you adopt me?'

'Shh.' Mrs Huifen kisses her head.

Trish pulls away.

She is comforted.

'I mean it.'

Mrs Huifen stands.

'I let you know in morning.' She chuckles. 'Such decisions require much sleep.'

Trish laughs and lies back as the old woman makes her way from the room.

There is a childlike sweetness about Trish now that makes her pretty. She sees beauty in ways she never thought possible. A beauty that went away from her world on a long pier over a placid lake ringed with trees.

METRO STREET VEHICLE – DAY

The drive into Pantheon is stunning.

Ethan drives the solar-powered utility shuttle, the

standard surface vehicle in Pantheon, along the main freeway directly into downtown. How they'd gotten it — *where* they'd gotten it, is yet another mystery. The same thing with her clothes. Size 7. They fit perfectly. Ethan was right about Jorlan. He seems to have infinite resources. She tugs at the strand of Mikimoto Akoya pearls he's included with the outfit he's selected for her. Not to mention exquisite taste.

The mysteries are compounding about him. Yet, as hard as she's tried, she still cannot read him.

A man of mystery.

She turns her eyes to the window.

The elevated Hyperloop trains slice the sky above them. Some slip along following the surface. Others are on radically different paths. Large sweeps dipping to the pavement then vaulting vertically only to dip again to the surface of another boulevard. Their velocity is phenomenal.

The buildings are mirror-like reflective — most shaped like inverted pyramids.

All glass in the metropolis is photo-electric. This city is directly from a science fiction writer's imagination.

There is no pollution.

The wide boulevards and buildings and perfectly manicured parks and walks look as if they were constructed within the last hour.

The solar electric surface vehicles are white — all the same — all made of amorphic, photovoltaic silicon.

They move along the elevated freeways at a precise velocity. There is no congestion. No Pantheon resident wastes valuable time commuting.

The metropolis is, in many ways, at least on the surface, an exemplary model of the city of the future. Unfortunately for the world, the future dropped in a little earlier than expected.

And came with drawbacks.

Those of value are cared for and live peaceful lives.

Those considered valueless are slated for submission.

Death from natural causes or death at their own hands. Everyone must be of value. There is zero tolerance. There are no exceptions. There are no infirm. There are no unhealthy. There are no aged. Vice is granted and controlled as long as it does not impair one's utility.

THE PRESIDENTIAL ESTATE

Once in front of the presidential estate, they wait at the curb behind a large bus of white and silver solar electric skin. A school group. It's perfect. An ideal diversion. Trish can mingle in with the group as if she is one of the teachers or chaperones.

It is 06:57, and the general is already on the steps with a young female colonel and two of his aides.

They are gazing off into the distance – fixated on a construction site.

They appear jovial.

Trish takes a breath.

'Jorlan wanted me to let you know that he decided on a slight modification of the plan.'

Trish stares Ethan in the eyes. 'What modification? What are you talking about?'

Ethan hands her the gun. The gun she was to use during the abduction. But things are wrong. From his look, she believes she understands.

'Jorlan thought abducting him – taking him with us is too…'

'…What are you saying, Ethan?'

He gives her a dark look.

'You're asking me to *kill him*?'

'It needs to be…'

'…But, why?'

'Look. He's the head of the military. He has their allegiance. Without him, and your sister gone, they'll be leaderless. Vulnerable.'

Trisha holds the gun and turns her eyes to the steps. She can't believe what they're asking of her. It's insane. Why didn't Jorlan tell me last night? Why had he instructed Ethan to wait until now? The last minute?

Again, she feels strange. As if Jorlan is…

She examines the gun.

Ethan is watching her.

She can feel his eyes as she turns it in her hands.

She looks again to the general.

Can I do this?

Walk up to him? Shoot him? And the others with him so I can make it back to the car?

Her mind is cluttered.

Am I now fully human? Can I actually violate the one element of our programming we retained when we became organic beings? *Kill?*

Kill… (she gazes at the people… humans, on the street) …Like *they* do?

Jorlan must have known all along.

And this is what he was preparing me for.

If he believes I can, and he's finally grown to love me, then… he believes in me. Then… perhaps I can…

She places the gun in her blazer pocket and reaches for the door.

She's decided.

'I'll be here.'

She stops and turns. 'Thank you, Ethan. Thank you for everything.'

He nods and watches as she leaves the car and takes to the steps.

OUTSIDE JORLAN'S ESTATE – NIGHT

Jorlan receives the news when Ethan returns. They stand together on the walk in front of his estate in the dark with rain falling from the elevated train.

Ethan tells him he is remorseful. Said Tess was like a

love-struck girl – doing something dangerous simply hoping to win his love. And because she'd convinced herself he was guiding her – in full belief she had become human enough to violate her programming. To do what humans have done to each other since the beginning. Something the AIs had decided they were above. Kill. Murder.

Jorlan shows compassion for him. Tells him he appreciates his feelings and wishes there had been another way.

They watch the aerial super-light universals – the Hyper-loops, in the distance shooting skyward then dipping between the buildings.

'Did you feel anything for her at all?'

Jorlan considers the question.

Thinks deeply about how he'd devised his plan, anticipated what TESS would do to try to reach him, and knew how he could manipulate her to fall in love with him.

He thinks of Ethan and knows how he will react to his answer. He has been loyal to him since the beginning. He will continue. Jorlan knows it is his nature. Regardless, whether he tells him the truth or not, he places a hand on his shoulder.

'Yes.'

Ethan shrugs. In reality, this is yet another part of Jorlan's business Ethan simply isn't curious about.

'I have your travel documents inside. You'll leave in an hour.'

Ethan nods and crosses the street to his car.

JORLAN'S ESTATE – NIGHT

After leaving Ethan, Jorlan makes his way through the galleries into the adjacent hotel. Now the residences.

He takes the lift to the 3rd floor and is soon standing inside his expansive suite. A series of rooms with the connecting walls removed, it is enormous and holds the most prized art pieces and sculpture in the world.

He stands in the middle of the main room gazing out the window at Pantheon.

It's white and silver lights are dazzling.

He actually feels stimulated watching it.

There's even an element of lust growing inside him that he barely understands.

'Is it over?'

He turns to Trish.

'Nearly.'

'They're both dead?'

'Yes.'

Trisha, in a loose cotton shirt and dark jeans holds his arm.

'You'll be able to reclaim another city.' She appears jubilant.

He's pensive and thoughtful with his hands prayer like beneath his chin.

'In time. There will be factions who are inured to this manifestation of a society. Harsh and autocratic as it may be, there are always those who will choose to see this as the answer.'

'But you *will* take it back.'

He smiles and holds her face. 'Of course we will. This will be our 3rd city.'

She kisses him.

He holds her in a passionate embrace.

Their lips are hesitant to part.

He pulls away slowly.

'Are you ready to do *your* part?' He smiles considering the irony. *'Madame President?'* She grimaces at the thought of what lie ahead for her now in Tess' role in the presidential estate. He holds his hand out, palm forward moving it from the neck of her shirt down to her jeans transforming them into the pyjamas Tess was typically seen wearing in the presidential estate. What the press was told she was wearing the night of her abduction. Her *staged* abduction three weeks earlier.

'Is this necessary?'

She looks down at her clothes and grimaces.

'I've had them looking for Tess all over the world. Following false leads. I believe only General Malik knew of the deception. Your creation's elaborate plan to find me by… by becoming you. To circumvent their suspicion that we exist, that I'm part of the resistance, they will need to find and rescue you where I last placed you.'

'Where?'

'The Middle East. The Arabian desert.'

She takes his hand and leans her head on his shoulder as they leave his private suite, the residences and make their way through the large dining room to the galleries.

'Ethan will take you. I've also arranged a little rebel pursuit to add a touch of reality to the show they'll broadcast to their citizenry. We want them back on our side, but we certainly don't want to see them lose faith in the justice system. We are certainly terrorists, but we are not anarchists.' He chuckles at his own wit. 'The transition will be difficult enough without adding that to the equation.'

They pass through one of the large glass walled corridors. Galleries on both sides. Archaeological artefacts. He pauses in front of a collection of Egyptian mummies and sarcophagi.

His face is strange. Analytical, but also displays searching.

A demon?

Could it be…?

He tilts his head and speaks. 'They thought they were making themselves eternal. Gods.'

'The Pharaohs?' Trish studies him.

'Yes.'

She continues watching while holding his hand but remains silent.

'I wonder if *your* pursuit… and all your AI technologists

are simply… simply after the same thing. Immortality. The quest for deification thinly veiled behind finely woven deception of scientific curiosity.'

They meet eyes.

'Will you grant me immortality so we can live together forever, Jorlan?'

His eyes close. A quiet moment passes. He opens them.

'No.' He shakes his head. 'Even if I could. I love you too much to curse you with such a meaningless existence.' He returns his gaze to the mummy. 'But then… perhaps existence itself *is* meaningless.'

He turns to her. His look is strange. They kiss and walk on through the galleries.

————

64

T. E. Mark's NOVELETTES

My Novelettes are a hybrid format designed to award the reader as close to a cinematic experience in story form as possible.

I've taken the pace and structure of a screenplay and combined these elements with the lengthier narrative structure of a short novella, or long short story. The Novelette.

Typically two-hour reads, the length of a full-length film, my Novella / Screenplay Novelettes move through scenes rather than chapters. This, I feel, increases the pace of the read and makes them more engaging.

I've tried to make each compelling and more complete than short stories while concentrating on theme, character development and story structure.

I hope I've succeeded in offering something new and valuable.

TE Mark - Writer / Screenwriter
Dec 2018

ABOUT THE AUTHOR

T. E. Mark is a Writer, Screenwriter and Violinist. He has studied Architecture, Music and Literature in the UK and in the US and has been penning stories since childhood with his first novel, Fractured Horizons, written in the wonderful city of Bath, England – also where the story is set.

Mark has written novels for young and adult readers and a selection of science articles for national and international magazines.

A MOMENT INTO THE SILENCE FELL was first published in 2018 as part of an anthology titled DREAMS INC. – The Novelettes of T. E. Mark – Vol II.

A MOMENT INTO THE SILENCE FELL the screenplay was also written by T. E. Mark.

Follow T. E. Mark at:
https://temarkauthor.wordpress.com
https://mthomasmark.wordpress.com
https://temarkurbanscratch.wordpress.com
temarkauthor@gmail.com